WELCOME TO THE WORLD OF Geronimo Stilton

GERONIMO
STILTON

Published by Sweet Cherry Publishing Limited
Unit 36, Vulcan House,
Vulcan Road,
Leicester, LE5 3EF,
United Kingdom

First published in the UK in 2018
2019 edition

2 4 6 8 10 9 7 5 3

ISBN: 978-1-78226-376-0

Text by Geronimo Stilton
Art Director: Iacopo Bruno
Graphic Designer: Laura Dal Maso / theWorldofDOT
Original cover illustration by Andrea Da Rold and Andrea Cavallini
Concept of illustration by Roberta Bianchi, produced by Valeria Turati, Andrea Da Rold and Andrea Cavallini with assistance from Lara Martinelli
Initial and final page illustrations by Roberto Ronchi and Ennio Bufi MAD5, Studio Parlapà and Andrea Cavallini. Map illustrations by Andrea Da Rold
Cover layout and typography by Elena Distefano
Interior layout and typography by Cecilia Bennett, Rhiannon Izard, Kellie Jones and Amy Wong
Graphics by Michela Battaglin

Original title: *Lo strano caso del fantasma al Grand Hotel*
Based on an original idea by Elisabetta Dami

www.geronimostilton.com/uk

Stilton is the name of a famous English cheese. It is a registered trademark of the Stilton Cheese Makers' Association. For more information go to www.stiltoncheese.com

www.sweetcherrypublishing.com

Printed and bound in India
I.IPP001

Geronimo Stilton

THIS HOTEL IS HAUNTED

Sweet Cherry
PUBLISHING

A Mysterious Ghost Story

Dear mouse friends, my name is Stilton, *Geronimo Stilton*. I am the editor of The Rodent's Gazette, the most famouse newspaper on Mouse Island. I'm also a writer by trade, and I love books.

I'm glad you're reading – I have a THRILLING new story to tell!

It all started one morning while I was having breakfast. As I poured a cup of PIPING HOT tea, I turned on the television.

THE RODENT'S GAZETTE

LATE-BREAKING NEWS!
LATE-BREAKING NEWS!
LATE-BREAKING NEWS!
LATE-BREAKING NEWS!
LATE-BREAKING NEWS!
LATE-BREAKING NEWS!

The newsmouse Pippi Skinnyfur announced, "Late-breaking news! We are here at New Mouse City's GRAND HOTEL, where all the guests are leaving because of a ghost!"

A ghost? I almost dropped my teacup. Had I heard right? Had she really said a ghost?

"Yes, that's right, you heard me, a ghost!" Ms. Skinnyfur continued.

"How strange!" I exclaimed. "Every mouse knows **THERE'S NO SUCH THING AS GHOSTS!**"

Behind Ms. Skinnyfur, rodents were scurrying out of the hotel. I could hear them squeaking, "We want our money back!"

Ms. Skinnyfur began interviewing the owner of the Grand Hotel, Horatzio

AS I WAS HAVING BREAKFAST ...
... I TURNED ON THE TV AND STARED.
A GHOST AT THE GRAND HOTEL?!

Hoteltail. "Mr. Hoteltail, a **creepy** ghost has been **HAUNTING** your hotel for about a month now. Is there anything you want to say to your guests?"

Poor Horatzio had tears in his eyes. "I want to extend a very sincere apology to our guests! I will refund all their money."

"What will become of the Grand Hotel? It's one of New Mouse City's most **beloved institutions**. Will it be forced to close?" Ms. Skinnyfur asked.

I turned off the television. The whole situation was strange.

I was concerned about poor Horatzio. He was an old friend of mine. Back in primary school, we used to spend our afternoons scampering around his family's hotel.

Back in School ...

When we were young mice, my friend Hercule Poirat and I always did our homework at Horatzio's.

We used to play hide and seek in the long corridors of the Grand Hotel.

Then we would have a snack in the hotel's enormouse kitchens ...

... and we'd hide all the room keys from the receptionist, Oswald Rattaldo!

Who? What? When? Where? Why?

When I left the house, I found a **surprise** waiting for me. On the doormat there was a letter addressed to me, *Geronimo Stilton*.

I was overcome with curiosity. I turned the package over and found a card that said:

Geronimo Stilton
8 Mouseford Lane
New Mouse City,
Mouse Island 19876
Go immediately to
The Grand Hotel.
Room number 313
has been reserved for you.
Wait for me there.
But do not squeak of this letter to
anyone (anyone at all)!

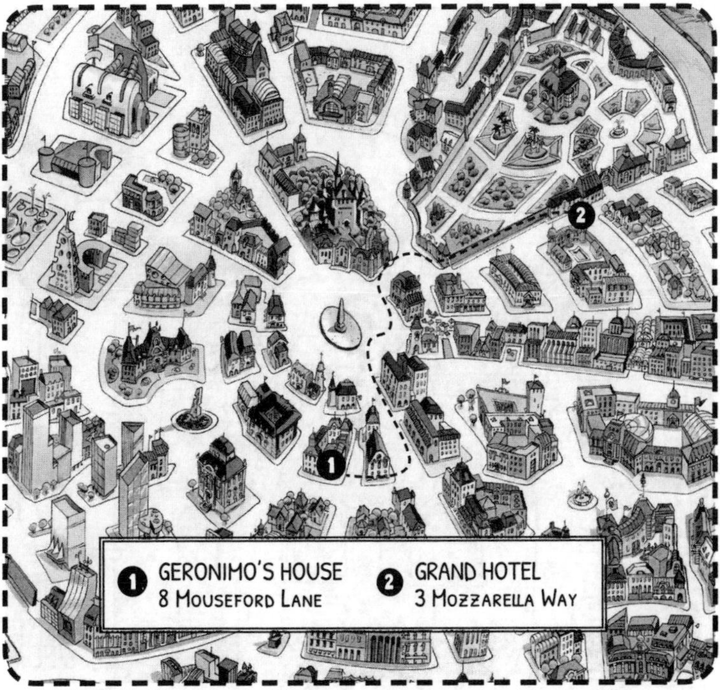

Perplexed, I put the letter back into its envelope. A million questions scampered through my mind.

WHO was inviting me to the Grand Hotel?

WHAT did the sender want from me?

WHEN had the mysterious invitation been sent?

WHERE had it come from?

And above all ... WHY?

GH
Grand Hotel
TAXI
TAXI

I was torn. I was intrigued by the letter, but I was also afraid of ghosts!

Eventually, curiosity won out. So I called a taxi to take me to the Grand Hotel.

When we arrived, a porter opened the door. "Welcome to New Mouse City's GRAND HOTEL!" he declared. His squeak sounded confident, but his whiskers were twitching nervously.

PORTER

AT LARGE HOTELS, THERE IS ALWAYS A UNIFORMED PORTER AT THE DOOR. THEY GREET GUESTS AS THEY ARRIVE AND CALL TAXIS FOR GUESTS WHO ARE LEAVING.

There was a crowd of rodents leaving the hotel. I was the only one who wanted to go in!

A mouse in her bathrobe ran out the door, screaming, **"I can't stay here a second longer!"**

I pushed through the revolving door and found myself in the lobby. The last of the guests were departing.

LOBBY

THE LOBBY IS THE HOTEL'S INDOOR ENTRANCE AREA. IN LARGE HOTELS, IT IS A VERY SPACIOUS AND ELEGANT ROOM WHERE YOU CAN FIND THE RECEPTION AND CHECKOUT DESKS AND THE CAFÉ.

1
2
3
7

5
4
6
1 - MAIN ENTRANCE
2 - CHECK-IN
3 - INFORMATION
4 - CHECKOUT
5 - RESERVATIONS
6 - LIFT
7 - CAFÉ

Room 313

I approached the reception desk, where **Oswald Rattaldo**, the receptionist, was seated. I noticed that his eyes were red, as if he had been **CRYING**.

A guest scurried past, yelling, "We want a full refund, do you hear me? I'd rather spend the night in a cat clinic than stay in this hotel another minute!"

"I'm sorry, sir, we have never had a ghost at the Grand Hotel before!" Oswald sighed.

RECEPTION

THE RECEPTION DESK IS IN THE LOBBY. IT'S WHERE GUESTS CHECK IN AND RECEIVE THEIR ROOM KEYS. WHEN IT'S TIME TO LEAVE, GUESTS COME HERE TO CHECK OUT AND ASK FOR THE BILL.

"Good morning,

Oswald, how are you?" I said. "I'm here for room 313."

Oswald recognised me immediately. "Mr. Geronimo! What a **pleasure** to see you again!" he said happily. "I see that suite 313 has been reserved in your name. Come, I will take you upstairs right away."

SUITE

SUITE IS A FRENCH WORD (PRONOUNCED 'SWEET') THAT MEANS 'SERIES OF ROOMS' OR 'APARTMENT'. A SUITE IS USUALLY MADE UP OF A BEDROOM, A BATHROOM, AND A SMALL LIVING ROOM.

Entering room 313 was like going back in time. Even though it had been years since I'd been inside the hotel, I remembered the canopy bed, the **Cheddar-coloured** carpet, and the golden cheese slice wallpaper.

I thanked Oswald for bringing me up. Then I went into the bathroom to wash my paws. Even the bathroom had remained the same. The only new detail I saw was the shower curtain, which was decorated with a pattern of bananas.

I frowned. That was a bit odd. Bananas?

That was when I heard a soft voice squeaking my name. *"Geronimoooo ..."*

I gulped. Could it be the ghost? No, it was probably just my overactive imagination.

I leaned over to turn on the tap. That was when I heard it again.

"Geronimoooo ..."

Strange!

I picked up the paw towel. Again I heard, *"Geronimoooo ..."*

Very strange!

Suddenly, the shower curtain began moving. Something inside it was reaching towards me! Its arms were open wide, like the tentacles of an **OCTOPUS**.

I was so scared, I could barely open my snout to squeak, "HEEEELLLLLLP!"

That was when a tail popped out from behind the curtain, then a paw, and finally a rat's snout. "*PEEKABOO!*"

I jumped backwards. "Wh-wh-who is it?"

A rodent with **GREY FUR** and whiskers shiny with fur gel poked his snout out.

"My dear Stilton, how did you like my little joke?"

Peekaboo!
Wh-wh-who is it?

he asked, smirking.

Only then did I recognise him. It was my friend Hercule Poirat! He's a detective, and loves mysteries the way mice love cheese.

Unfortunately for me, he also loves playing jokes. And I'm his favourite target! (It's not my fault I'm a 'fraidy mouse.)

I should've realised something was up when I saw that banana-patterned shower curtain. Hercule just loves bananas ... **and he knows how much I detest them!**

Strange Things Are Happening at the Grand Hotel!

"What are you doing here, Hercule?" I demanded.

"Strange things are happening at the Grand Hotel," he replied seriously. "Scrape the **cheese** out of your ears, Stilton! Even a scaredy-mouse like you knows that ghosts don't exist. So who has been **terrorising** the guests at this hotel for the last month?"

Then he lowered his squeak. "I need your help to find out!"

I sighed. "Hercule, you know that I'm a very busy mouse. I have a new book to write, and –"

"I'm begging you, my dear Stilton!"

Hercule cried. "If you don't want to do it for me, do it for our city! The GRAND HOTEL is a beloved New

Mouse City establishment, and that is precious. Think about how many rodents work at the Grand Hotel. You don't want them to lose their jobs, do you? Plus, we simply *must* help our old friend Horatzio! He needs us."

Then he lit up. "I have a ***GENIUS*** idea! Let's go to him now! He will convince you!"

Before I could protest, **he was dragging me to Horatzio's office.**

A Great Love Story!

We found Horatzio at his desk, **SOBBING**. "Oh, my dear friends, whatever will I do? I'll be forced to sell my hotel! For generations this hotel has belonged to my family. Ahh, **WHAT A CAT-ASTROPHE!**"

"Come on, Horatzio, take a tissue." Hercule consoled him. "Have no fear, Hercule Poirat is here! Your old friend Geronimo and I will help you. Please calm down. We need to ask you some questions."

Horatzio brightened up at once. "Really? You'll really help me?"

I sighed. You see, I truly am a **busy mouse**. I have stories to edit and deadlines to meet and a newspaper to put out. But I simply can't refuse a friend in need!

I took out a notebook and began jotting down some notes. "Tell us everything, starting from the beginning."

Horatzio pointed at a painting behind his desk. It depicted a CURLY-whiskered rodent and an **elegant**, smiling female rodent.

"Do you remember these mice, Geronimo? They are my great-grandparents Everest and Arabella Hoteltail. They were the ones who founded New Mouse City's Grand Hotel years and years ago. Theirs was **a great love story** – oh, how they loved each other!

Everest and Arabella Hoteltail

EVEREST AT WORK

"My great-grandfather was a **bricklayer**, and my great-grandmother was a cook. They were poor, but full of energy and enthusiasm. Everest decided to build a hotel brick by brick. And guests came from all over Mouse Island to taste Arabella's **delicious dishes**."

Horatzio took a deep breath and then went on. "My great-grandparents loved making travellers happy. Inviting them to enjoy hot meals and comfortable beds was their life's work!

ARABELLA IN THE KITCHEN

"Over the years, the hotel got bigger. It became the most famouse hotel in the

The Grand Hotel back in the time of Horatzio's great-grandparents

city, and then on all of Mouse Island. But now this ghost is ruining me! Soon I will be forced to sell the hotel to that awful rodent ..."

My ears perked up. "Someone wants you to sell the hotel? Who?"

"A mysterious businessmouse, **Bradley Bigbottom**. For a month now, he has been asking me to sell it to him at a really, really low price. And now it seems I have no choice, with this ghost wandering the halls for the past month. All the guests have been complaining and fleeing the hotel! And do you know what that **SLIMY SEWER RAT** wants to do to my hotel? He wants to turn it into a ...

TOILET FACTORY!

Hercule was outraged. "A toilet factory? Never! They'll have to **FLUSH** us out of here first! Isn't that right, my dear Stilton? Did you get my little joke? Flush us out of here ... get it?"

I just rolled my eyes. I was too busy thinking about what Horatzio had said to laugh at Hercule's silly pun. For a month a *mysterious* rodent had been asking Horatzio to sell ...

For a month a ghost had wandered around the hotel ...

For a month all the **guests** had complained.

A month?

A month?

A month?

The Secrets of the Grand Hotel

I turned to Horatzio. "Please show us where, how, and when this ghost appears!"

Horatzio nodded and picked up a set of keys. "I'll take you on a tour of the whole hotel while we talk."

As he led us down a hallway, he continued with his tale. "Many mice have seen a ghost here. The first ones to complain were guests who come to our hotel regularly, Count and Countess von Ratsis. They were returning to their room after a reception at Countess de Snobberella's castle when they found themselves

COUNT AND COUNTESS VON RATSIS

snout-to-snout with the ghost!"

"**BLISTERING BANANAS!** I guess this ghost doesn't appear for just any old rat," Hercule exclaimed.

"Then he scared the entire Rodentine family," Horatzio went on. "Those poor mice! Oswald saw them leave in a hurry, with looks of **HORROR** frozen onto their snouts. Then, a few days later, two elderly mice saw the ghost while they were getting out of the lift ..."

THE RODENTINE FAMILY

As Horatzio continued his tale, we toured the Grand Hotel from the cellar to the attic. **It was huge!**

GH
Grand H

WHO SAW THE GHOST?

Finally, we came back to the lobby. "We would like to talk to all the ladies and gentlemice who work at the Grand Hotel," Hercule announced. Horatzio answered sadly, "Please feel free to interview them – the ones who remain, that is. Many of our employees have also been scared away by the ghost."

At the entrance to the hotel, we found Oswald again. "What a shame to lose this precious landmark, Mr. Geronimo," he said gravely. "The **GRAND HOTEL** is the heart of our city."

"We will do everything we can to help Horatzio," I assured him. "But tell me, **have you seen the ghost?**"

Oswald shook his snout. "No, he never passed by me.

But many guests have described him to me – they say he glows in the dark!"

I jotted down what he'd said in my notebook: glows in the dark.

Next we went to look for the housekeeper, Matilda Broommouse. We checked in the housekeeping headquarters, but we didn't see her anywhere – until we heard someone **SOBBING** in the broom cupboard.

I kissed her paw in greeting. (I am a real gentlemouse!) "Good day, Miss Broommouse. Why are you crying?"

"I-I-I don't want to lose my job," she stammered.

"Do not worry, Miss Broommouse, we are on the case!" Hercule assured her. "Tell me, have you seen the ghost? When? And what were you doing?"

She sobbed. "I saw him coming down the stairs ... *Sigh* ... He scared all the guests away!" Then she screamed, **"Look!** Another spiderweb! Since the ghost has been here, I keep finding them all over, even if I **dust** every day. I do a good job, please tell Horatzio that! It's not my fault the guests keep running away."

"Calm down, dear Miss Broommouse, the hotel is in good paws! We will save it," Hercule responded.

In my notebook I wrote: spiderwebs.

Then we went to see the hotel's cook, Sergio Creampuff. We found him in the kitchen, seated in front of the stove. "Who would have thought that the Grand Hotel would close after so many years?" he sighed.

"Have you ever seen the ghost?" I asked.

"Yes, every time a guest saw the ghost, it would

Sergio Creampuff

also appear in the kitchen. It was **BIG** and **tall**, with creepy clanking armour and chains."

"Have you noticed anything else strange?" I asked. "I mean, besides the fact that there seems to be a ghost."

The cook pulled on his whiskers thoughtfully. "Weeeelll, there is something, now that you mention it. For a month now, all the guests have been complaining about finding white fur in their soup. But no one here in the kitchen has white fur! Also, I keep finding chocolate wrappers on the floor, but no one in the kitchen eats chocolates."

I jotted down big, tall, chains, white fur, chocolate wrappers.

Jack Joltson

We said goodbye to Sergio and went to the hotel's basement to look for the ELECTRICIAN, Jack Joltson. We found him changing a lightbulb.

Hercule and I introduced ourselves. Jack was very happy that someone was investigating the strange situation at the Grand Hotel.

"Have you seen the ghost or noticed anything strange since the ghost first appeared?" I asked him.

"I haven't seen the ghost," Jack said. "But there is one thing I don't understand. Ever since the hotel started being haunted, I keep hearing **eerie** violin music. But the hotel isn't wired with a stereo system!"

I nodded and jotted what he'd said in my notebook: violin music.

Hercule winked. "This ghost is brainier than a lab rat! But it's only a matter of time before we unmask him, right, my dear Stilton?"

Next we needed to find Casey Valise, the head porter. But there weren't any more guests around for him to help, and no one knew where he had gone.

We decided to go back to see Oswald. We found Casey keeping him company at the reception desk.

Casey LIT UP when he saw us. "Can I carry a bag for you, sir?"

I smiled warmly. "No thank you, Casey. But I would like to ask you a question. Have you seen the ghost?"

Casey pulled out a bright plastic ring and began to fiddle with it. "I'm not sure I've seen him. But I did find this one evening. Do you think it might be a clue?"

As I reached out to take it, I noticed that it was glowing. Hmm ... could it belong to the ghost?

I jotted down plastic ring, glows in the dark.

Finally, we went to the Grand Hotel's main office to meet the hotel's director, Ms. Bertha. We entered a very elegant room that smelled of **EXPENSIVE** perfume. I knew the scent quite well – it was the same one worn by my arch-nemesis, Sally Ratmousen, the editor of *The Daily Rat*. That odour was enough to send a shiver down my tail.

The room was filled with precious objects: embroidered silk pillows, antique furniture, paintings by famouse artists.

Ms. Bertha was standing at her desk. She was tall and a bit stout and dressed beautifully in a very **elegant** black suit. Her paws glittered with jewellery.

Ms. Bertha looked at us and sighed. "Oh, I am so sorry that the Grand Hotel has to close!" I also heard her mumble under her breath, "Nothing lasts forever!"

"And what will you do when the GRAND HOTEL

closes, Ms. Bertha?" I asked her.

"Oh, a manager like me will have options, of course," she said proudly. "Why, I've already been offered a position as director of a **TOILET FACTORY** ... um, I mean, I will certainly find another job. With my experience, I won't have any trouble! But now, please excuse me. I must get back to work. There is so much to do these days!"

So Hercule and I left her office and went looking for Horatzio. We wanted to fill him in on everything we'd learned from his employees.

We found him in the lift, and together we returned to room 313. As Hercule slid the key into the lock, he commented, "It was quite interesting to listen to everyone's stories, wasn't it, my dear Stilton? **Let's review our notes all together and see if we can deduce anything!**"

312
313

A Genius Idea!

As we entered the suite, Hercule exclaimed, "I have a *GENIUS IDEA*! Tonight we will sleep here! Alone! And we will give that ghost the surprise of his life (or death, as the case may be)! What do you think, my dear Stilton? Isn't that a genius idea?"

I'll be honest with you, dear reader. I thought it was a **terrible idea**! As you know, I'm quite a 'fraidy mouse. The last thing I wanted was to spend the night in a haunted hotel.

"Umm, sleep here tonight?" I mumbled. "To surprise the ghost? What if *he's* the one that surprises *us*?"

"Maybe it would be safer if I stayed here, too," Horatzio proposed.

"My dear Horatzio, that is very kind of you, but it is totally unnecessary! We aren't afraid!" Hercule replied. "Are we, Stilton?"

"N-n-nooo, I-I'm not s-s-scared," I stammered. "But if Horatzio insists–"

Hercule cut me off. "It's okay, Horatzio. Why don't you leave us to our work now? Oh, but before you go, I would like to get some room service. Here's my order:

1 large bunch of bananas!

1 banana-flavoured fondue!

5 banana cream pies!

6 banana splits!

8 pounds of candied bananas!

10 jars of banana jam!

4 large pizzas with bananas on top!

4 extra-large banana smoothies!

10 banana-nut muffins!

5 boxes of banana-flavoured chocolates!"

"You see, solving mysteries always makes me hungry,

BANANAS!
BANANA-FLAVOURED FONDUE!
BANANA CREAM PIE!
BANANA SPLITS!
CANDIED BANANAS!
BANANA JAM!
PIZZA WITH BANANAS ON TOP!
BANANA SMOOTHIES!
BANANA-NUT MUFFINS!
BANANA-FLAVOURED CHOCOLATES!

and my brain works better when my stomach is full … of bananas! Hmm, better make it two bunches of bananas – no, how about three? You never know when you might need a little extra BRAIN POWER!"

Hercule exclaimed. "We're going to stay up all night, listening for the ghost to howl, *'Oooooooooooh … '"*

I shivered. "The ghost howls?"

"I don't know if it howls, but it sounded spooky, didn't it?" Hercule snickered. "My dear Stilton, you should see how PALE you've gone. Is something bothering you?"

"Pale? I'm pale all right!" I shrieked. "**I CAN'T TAKE IT ANYMORE!** I'm out of here!"

"Please stay, Geronimo!" Horatzio begged me as he left. "If you and Hercule don't solve this mystery, I'm ruined!"

Soon, Horatzio returned with waiters bringing all the food Hercule had ordered. As soon as Hercule had his paws on the bananas, he tossed Horatzio and the waiters out like yesterday's cheese rinds. "Shoo! Everyone out now! Let me work!"

Then he hung a sign on the door:

A Ghastly Night

As soon as everyone was gone, Hercule lit two candles, turned off the lights, and whispered, "And now, we wait."

"Wait for what?" I whispered back.

"Wait for the ghost to show his snout!" Hercule HISSED.

"Maybe he won't come ..." I whispered hopefully.

"Noooo, I'm certain he'll appear," Hercule hissed.

"Why did you light candles instead of turning on the light?" I whispered.

"Candles add a bit of mystery. You like *mysteries*, don't you, my dear Stilton?" he whispered.

"No, I don't like mysteries!" I whispered vehemently. "You know very well that I am a complete scaredy-mouse! Why are we whispering?"

"Because in plaaaaces where there are ghoooooosts, one should never squeak looooooudly ..." Hercule whispered. His squeak was quite creepy.

That was it. I lost my cheese. "**I CAN'T TAKE IT ANYMORE!**" I shouted.

Hercule just looked at me sympathetically. You really are quite a scaredy-mouse."

At that moment, the door burst open ...

"**Aaaaaaaaack!**" I screamed in terror. "It's the **GHOOOOOOOOOOOST!**"

But it was only Horatzio. "Sorry, friends, I didn't

mean to scare you! I just wanted to warn you that the phone lines have suddenly gone down."

I was so embarrassed. "Oh yes ... um ... I ... I was just doing some tests so we'd be ready when the ghost appears ..." I stammered.

"Ha ha ha!" Hercule laughed. "You were testing your scream of terror!"

"Goodnight, my friends!" Horatzio said.

I sighed. **I had a sinking feeling that the night would be ghastly!**

IIIIIII'M THE GHOOOOOST ...

Hercule **plopped** onto the bed and sank into the FEATHER PILLOWS. Then he opened the mini-fridge with the tip of his tail and took out a cheeseshake. With one paw, he sampled a banana-flavoured chocolate, and with the other he turned on the TV.

"Look on the bright side, my dear Stilton. Here we

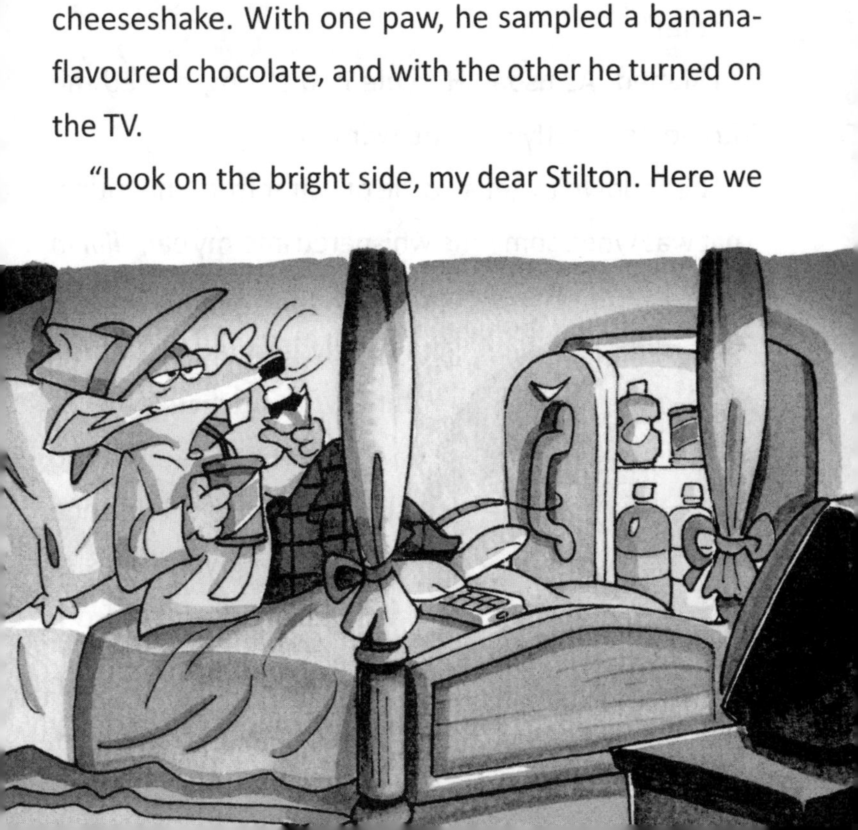

are in the most **luxurious** hotel in all of New Mouse City ... for free! We've got silk sheets, feathery pillows, a mini-fridge filled with the finest cheesy beverages and snacks, plus all the TV stations you could ever want! It's positively banana-rific!"

I shivered. "Unfortunately, the service also includes a ghost!"

"Pshaw!" Hercule scoffed. "This ghost is nothing a **whisker-licking-good** investigator like me can't handle!"

I sighed. As usual, Hercule had strong-pawed me into doing exactly what he wanted.

I bent down to get a bottle of water from the fridge. That was when someone whispered into my ear, *"IIIII'm the ghoooooost ..."*

I nearly jumped out of my fur. "Who said that? H-help!"

It was Hercule. "Did you like my little joke? Hee hee hee! Scaring you is easier than taking a banana from a **baby mouseling**!"

That was the last slice of cheese, as far as I was concerned. "**I CAN'T TAKE IT ANYMORE!**" I shrieked.

I scampered into the bathroom, but as soon as I went in, the lights clicked off.

Someone howled, *"IIIIII'm the ghoooooooost ..."*

"Wh-who is that?" I squeaked. "H-help!"

It was Hercule, of course. He turned the lights back on. He was rolling on the floor, laughing. "Hee hee hee, you should see yourself, Stilton! Your tail is all **TWISTED UP** from fright!"

Exasperated, I went out onto the balcony to get some air. But the curtain behind me shook as a ghostly voice howled, *"Ooooooh, did you*

thiiiiink you could hiiiiiide?"

"HEEELLLLLLP!" I screamed in terror.

Naturally, it was Hercule again. "You can't even tell the difference between a curtain and a ghost, can you, my dear Stilton?" He snickered. "Hmph, you're so easy to scare, it's no fun playing pranks on you!"

At that moment, the lights went out!

"Enough with the tricks, Hercule!" I screamed. "Turn the lights back on!"

"B-but I didn't turn them off!" he stammered.

"Stop playing around, Poirat!"

"I-I-I'm telling you I didn't turn off the light!" Hercule exclaimed.

The blood froze in my veins. **"Well, if you didn't, then who did?"**

THEN WHO DiD?
THEN WHO DiD?
THEN WHO DiD?
THEN WHO DiD?

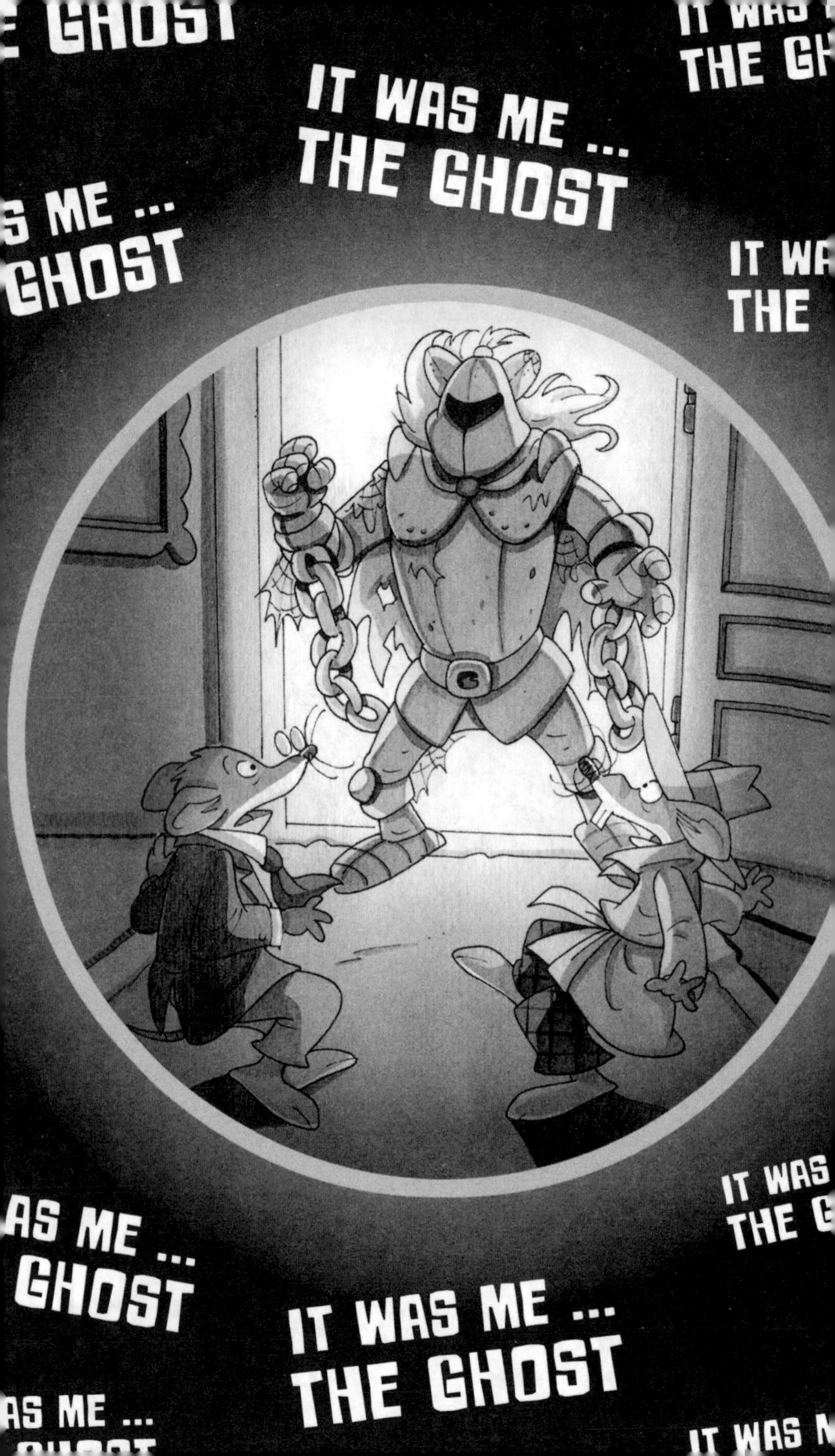
IT WAS ME ...
THE GHOST
IT WAS ME ...
THE GHOST

Do You Think That Was the Ghost?

A key turned in the lock, and the door to our suite burst open.

A spine-chilling squeak howled, *"It was meeeeee ... The ghoooooost!"*

Hercule and I were so terrified we screeched: **"HEEEEEEEEEELLLLLLLLLLLLLP!** HEEEEEEEEEEELLLLLLLLLLLLLP!"

In the dark, we saw a glowing ghostly figure dressed in heavy armour draped in spiderwebs. Thick white **FUR** poked out from under his helmet.

The ghost was dragging long, **glowing** chains behind him ... but they didn't make any noise! Instead, I heard violin music that seemed to come from far away. It was a creepy tune that sent a **chill** down my tail.

The ghost waved its chains in the air and howled,

"GEEEEEEEETTTTT OUT OF HEEEEERE, ALLLLL OF YOOOUUUU! THIS IS MYYYYYY HOTELLLLL. GEEEEEEETTTT OUUUUUUUT!"

Then he gave a gloomy cackle and left, slamming the door behind him. A moment later, the lights clicked back on. I took a deeeeeeeeeep breath and realised ... I was all alone! "Poirat! Hercule Poirat, where are you?"

A tiny squeak whispered from the far side of the suite: "I'm over here, my dear Stilton!"

Hercule was whiter than mould on Brie. He scrambled out of his hiding place and peeled a banana with trembling paws.

"I'm going to need the power of potassium to get through this!" he said. "Well, what do you think, my dear Stilton? Was that the ghost?"

I nodded. "I was so scared my tail is in tangles," I muttered.

"Ohh, yes, yes ... he was truly t-terrifying!" Hercule stammered. "I was scared myself. Please forgive me for poking fun at you before."

I gave him a hearty slap on the tail. "Don't worry about it! Anyone can get scared. The important thing is to try to overcome your fears."

Then I told him what Aunt Sweetfur always used to tell me: **"Never let fear conquer your love of adventure!"**

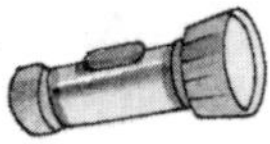

Never Let Fear Conquer Your Love of Adventure!

"'Never let fear conquer your love of adventure!'" Hercule repeated. "**BURNT BANANA BREAD!** Your aunt is a really intelligent rodent!"

He threw away his banana peel and repeated, "Never let fear conquer your love of adventure! I'm not afraid of the ghost (since ghosts don't exist), and I'm not even afraid of the **dark!** But most of all, I'm not afraid

because I'm not alone. I have a dear friend with me. And we will help each other be brave!"

With that, he grabbed a torch and scurried towards the door.

"Follow me, my dear Stilton. Let's reveal the mouse behind the mask! By the time we're through with him, the only place he'll be shaking his chains is in **RATCATRAZ PRISON!**"

"You said it, Poirat! I'm right behind you," I declared.

Together, we hurried down the dark corridor.

Someone Went Through Here ...

In the distance, we heard a loud *BANG*.

Strange ... There wasn't anyone at the end of the corridor!

We inspected the walls, looking for some sort of secret passage, but we didn't find anything that looked like a door.

"**Where could the ghost have gone?**" I murmured, shivering. "He seems to have disappeared, almost as if he went right through the wall." I remembered Aunt Sweetfur's advice. "There's no such thing as ghosts ... There's no such thing as ghosts ..." I murmured, trying to reassure myself.

I was still looking for clues when suddenly Hercule called, "**Yoo-hoo!** Over here! I think I've found something, my dear Stilton!"

He showed me an air-conditioning grate that was slightly crooked. There was a screw on the floor, as if someone had tried to put the grate back on in a hurry.

"Someone went through here," Hercule muttered. "And it wasn't a ghost, or my name isn't Hercule Poirat!"

We opened the air-conditioning grate. Inside, we found pawprints that **glowed** in the dark!

"How strange!" I said.

"Yes," said Hercule, nodding sagely. "One doesn't usually see pawprints in air-conditioning ducts ... especially not glowing pawprints!"

I remembered that the ghost had been glowing when we'd seen him. A **LIGHTBULB** went off in my brain. These pawprints might be from glow-in-the-dark paint!

I told Hercule my theory. "Let's follow the prints!" he declared.

We crawled into the air-conditioning duct. It was so

narrow that we had to continue on all fours. Hercule bumped into me, and I **BANGED** my snout on the top of the duct.

"Be careful now, my dear Stilton!" Hercule said, chuckling. "You don't want to damage your little grey cells, now do you?"

"They're probably already damaged – by fear. **I CAN'T TAKE IT ANYMORE!**" I shrieked.

Hercule pinched my tail. "My dear Stilton, you're more skittish than a kitten in a dog kennel. Calm down!"

SECOND CLUE!

Right then, I noticed something weird: the air-conditioning duct was full of **spiderwebs**.

Strange! There shouldn't be any spiderwebs in an air-conditioning duct.

I remembered something Matilda Broommouse had told us. She'd said that since the ghost had started appearing, she'd spotted spiderwebs all over the hotel.

We crawled along till the duct ended, and we found ourselves in the kitchen. On the floor in front of us was a pile of chocolate wrappers.

Strange! Ghosts don't eat chocolates.

But I remembered that Sergio Creampuff kept finding chocolate wrappers in the kitchen.

We followed the pawprints all the way to a door. We opened it ... and discovered a staircase!

We followed the tracks up the stairs until we found ourselves in front of a little door.

Of course ... It was the entrance to the **ATTIC**! Horatzio had shown it to us during our tour.

Hercule and I exchanged glances. Then we opened the door.

It was dark inside the attic, and it smelled of mould, dust, and forgotten objects. At one end there was an old canopy bed with **MOTH-EATEN CURTAINS**. In the corners stood decrepit, unwanted items: paintings with chipped frames, beaten-up old lamps, mouldy pillows with ripped linings. But there wasn't a soul anywhere, not even a mouse.

I reached under the bed to make sure no one was hiding there. My paw touched something with long fur.

"AAAAAAAAAAAAAAAAAAACK! A CAT!!!" I screamed.

I was about to faint from fright when I heard Hercule chuckling. "That's no cat! It's just a white wig."

Strange! I had never seen a white wig around the Grand Hotel before.

Then I remembered that guests had complained to Sergio Creampuff about white fur they'd found in their soup.

I gathered my courage and continued exploring the attic. I noticed a tall wardrobe and decided to check it out. When I opened it, I found armour!

Strange! I had never seen any armour in the hallways of the Grand Hotel.

Then I remembered the ghost we had seen was

wearing armour.

Suddenly, some chains that had been resting on top of the wardrobe fell onto my snout!

Strange! The chains bounced right off me ... because they were made of plastic!

Then I remembered that Casey Valise had found a plastic ring after the ghost had appeared.

Hercule and I kept searching for clues. We soon discovered an air-conditioning duct in the attic with a portable stereo inside. I pushed play, and **gloomy** violin music filled the air.

Strange! An air-conditioning duct was an unusual place to put a portable stereo.

Then I remembered that Jack Joltson had said he kept hearing strange music.

"Spiderwebs ... chocolates ... a white wig ... armour

... chains ... music ... we found it all!" Hercule declared. "Everything except the glow-in-the-dark paint."

At that moment, I accidentally stepped into a can of glowing paint. "I found that, too, Hercule!" I exclaimed.

"That does it, my dear Stilton!" Hercule declared. "***This phantom is a big, fat phoney!*** Some trickster has been dressing up as a ghost!"

"We've got to find him!" I shouted, and stroked my snout thoughtfully. **"I think I know someone who might be able to help us."**

A Little Help from a Friend

First thing the next morning, Hercule and I strolled into **TRICKS FOR TAILS**, a joke shop on Fastrat Lane. The owner, Paws Prankster, was a good friend of my cousin Trap.

"Hiya, Geronimo!" Paws shouted from the back. "How are you?"

"I'm fine," I replied. "But I'm looking for something special –"

Before I could finish squeaking, I felt something **FURRY** tickling my neck.

"Heeeeellllllllp! A spider!" I screamed.

Then I realized that it was merely one of Paws's pranks. The spider was actually a **RUBBER TOY**!

"Funny, very funny," I muttered. "But I'd really like to talk to you about serious business ..."

That was when I felt something slimy under my paw.

"Heeeelllllllp! A snake!" I yelled.

Then I realised that it was another trick.

As Paws and Hercule giggled, I tried to continue. "I want to ask y –"

Suddenly, a SKULL on a shelf lit up. Its teeth chattered as it howled, "Howdy, Cheeseheads!"

"HEEEELLLLLLLLLP!" I squealed. "A talking skull!"

But it was yet another one of Paws's gags.

"**I CAN'T TAKE IT ANYMORE!**" I yelped in exasperation. "Hercule, for the love of all that's cheesy and delicious, we need to get serious if we want to solve the case of the ghost at the GRAND HOTEL!"

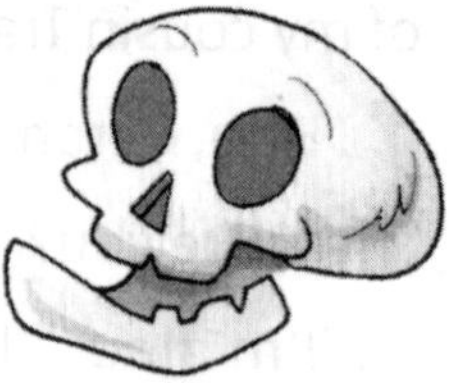

Paws stopped giggling at once. "A ghost at the Grand Hotel? I'm sorry to hear that it's in trouble. It is one of the **finest establishments** in New Mouse City. Tell me what I can do to help."

Hercule perked up his ears and began interrogating him. "We need some information, if you please!

Has a mouse come in recently and purchased any of the following?"

Paws checked his records carefully.

1. Glow-in-the-dark paint
2. Fake spiderwebs
3. Chocolates
4. A white wig
5. Fake armour
6. Plastic chains
7. A violin music recording

"Yes, there was a rodent who came in here and bought almost all those things – everything except for the chocolates. This is a **JOKE** store, not a sweet shop!"

"Describe this mouse for me. Was he very very tall or very very short? Very very **FAT** or very very THIN?" Hercule asked.

Paws stroked his snout thoughtfully. "He was **SHORT**, and quite THIN. He was wearing a light grey suit – no, actually it was black and pinstriped. His shirt was a loud colour – I think it was yellow – and his tie was embroidered with the letters *B.B.* He was a very flashy mouse and he was covered with jewellery. He had gold buttons on his jacket and a diamond ring as big as a ball of mozzarella. His shoes were also really **Shiny**, and he kept chewing on chocolates. When he left, I had to sweep up a bunch of empty wrappers off the floor."

Hercule was perplexed. "There's just one small fly in the **FONDUE**. Our trickster ghost is big and tall, but this rodent is short and thin."

I nodded. "Paws, any idea how we could find the rodent who came in here?"

"I saw him head towards the harbour in a **fancy** stretch limousine," Paws replied.

We thanked Paws for his help and scurried out of the store.

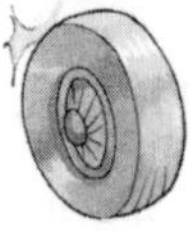

Only the Finest for Our B.B.!

As soon as we left the store, we climbed onto the bananacycle (Hercule's motorcycle) and **ZOOMED** off towards the harbour. We circled around for a while, but our patience paid off: we spotted a huge, flashy limousine as long as a bus. There was no mistaking it! Everything was made of **SOLID GOLD**, even

the tyres. It **SHONE** in the sun like a sweaty slice of Swiss cheese.

Hercule slid on a pair of dark sunglasses. "That thing's so bright I need to wear shades!"

The driver – a rodent as tall as a door, as wide as a wardrobe, and as threatening as a **MOUNTAIN LION** – climbed out of the limo, leaving the door open behind him.

"I have a genius idea. I will investigate the limo!" Hercule declared.

"Stop it, Poirat! ***Are you crazy?***" I cried.

Before I could stop him, he'd disappeared inside the vehicle, squeaking, "I just want to take a look. I'll be right back, I promise!"

I followed him with a sigh. The inside of the limousine was even more extraordinary than the outside. The steering wheel was solid gold, with the initials *B.B.* engraved in the centre. Behind the front seat was a large area that held little yellow sofas. The initials B.B. were embroidered on everything!

Hercule spotted a control panel and murmured,

"I wonder what all these buttons are for."

"No! Hercule! Don't touch those!"

But it was too late – he had already pressed one of the buttons. With a loud buzz, a big cabinet slid open. Inside were an enormouse television and a stereo so big it looked like it belonged in a dance club.

Hercule pressed another button, and a golden **HOT TUB** in the shape of a **B** appeared. It had a solid-gold tap.

He pressed another button, and a B-shaped bed slid down. Another button opened a closet in the shape of a B. It was filled with designer suits, ties, and hats.

Finally, Hercule put his paw on a button that opened a B-shaped refrigerator. It was fully stocked with the **finest cheeses**!

Hercule immediately began rummaging through the refrigerator. "Wow, triple-cheese chocolates and aged Cheddar – only the finest for our B.B.!"

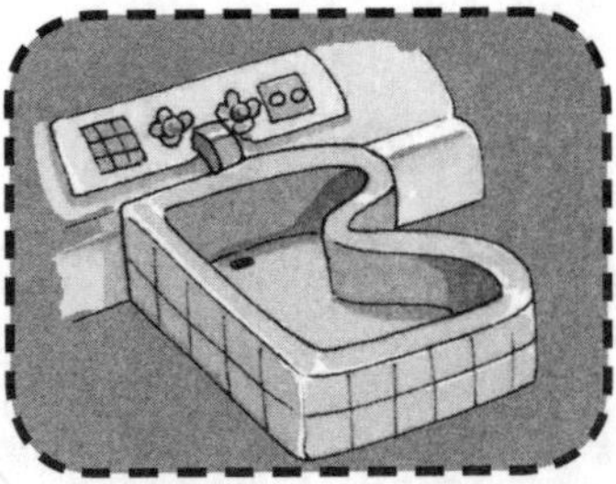

Suddenly, I realised that someone was coming. I immediately recognised the approaching mouse from Paws's description. It was him. ***It was B.B.!***

He flung open the front door to the limo and scurried in, followed by his driver. Meanwhile, Hercule and I were hiding right behind them in the backseat! We grabbed each other's paws and held on for dear life as the limo's engine started. We were moving!

B.B. pulled a golden mobile phone out of his pocket and started to make a phone call.

"Hello? It's me. I have good news for you, Sleezer!"

B.B.'s Stretch Limo

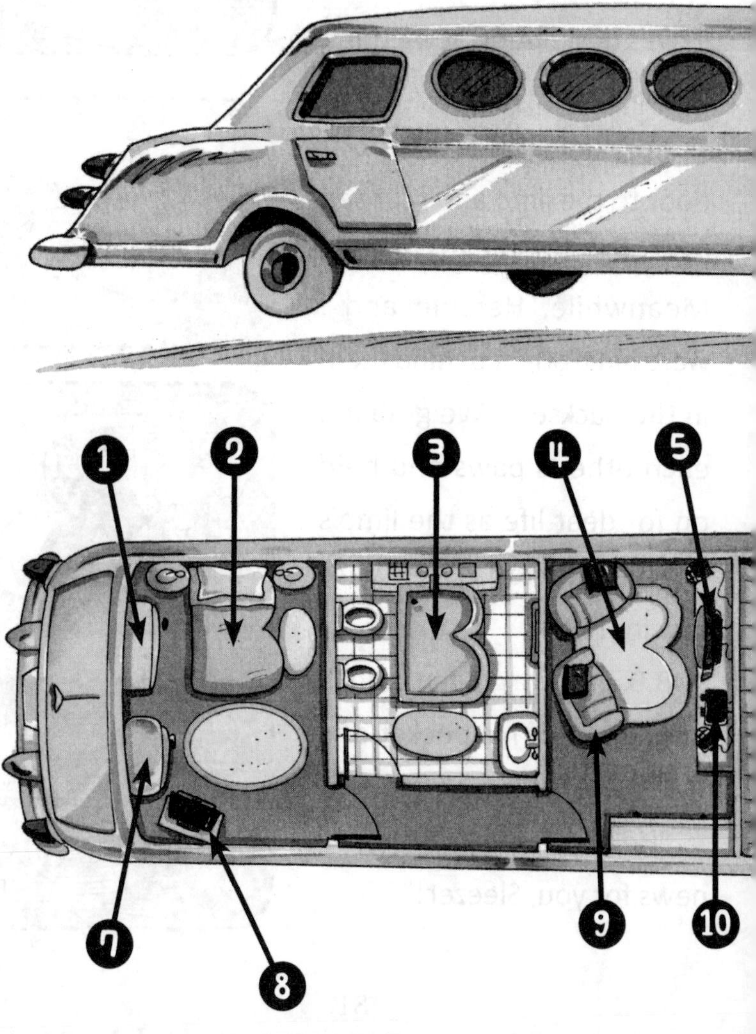

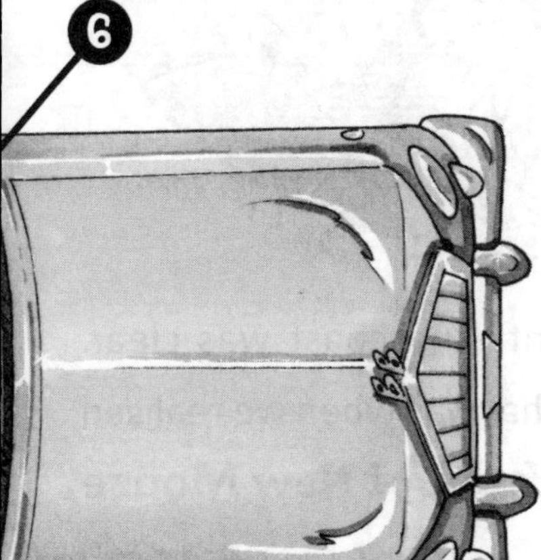

1 - WARDROBE
2 - BED
3 - HOT TUB
4 - CARPET
5 - GIANT TELEVISION
6 - FRONT SEAT
7 - REFRIGERATOR
8 - SMALLER TELEVISION
9 - SOFAS
10 - STEREO

Hearing that name sent chills down my tail. Do you remember **Sleezer**? That good-for-nothing sewer rat is always trying to take over New Mouse City!

I wanted to hear more of B.B.'s phone call, but unfortunately, the gigantic limo stopped and B.B. got out, followed by his driver.

Hercule and I waited until the coast was clear. Then we climbed out, too. That was when we realised **that we were right in front of New Mouse City's Grand Hotel!**

B.B. Stands for ... Bradley Bigbottom!

B.B. strode into the GRAND HOTEL like he owned the place. Only then did I get a good look at him. He was wearing a black pinstriped suit with golden buttons, with a white and yellow silk shirt underneath, and a flashy tie with the initials *B.B.* on it. On one paw he had a **DIAMOND RING** the size of a Cheesy Chew. His orange shoes were very shiny, as if someone had waxed them with butter. He was wearing dark sunglasses and a large-brimmed hat. His whiskers glistened with fur wax. He was surrounded by a cloud of cologne that was stinkier than blue cheese.

B.B. was picking his teeth with an ivory toothpick. He withdrew it and said to Horatzio, "So? Have you decided to sell?"

I took a step forwards. "My name is Stilton, *Geronimo*

Stilton," I said. "I haven't yet had the pleasure of meeting you, sir, but there is something that I would like to say to you. Not everything has a price tag. You can't buy love, friendship, freedom, or peace. The best things in life are **PRICELESS!** And among the many things that cannot be bought are the history and tradition of Mouse Island and its long-standing institutions. New Mouse City's Grand Hotel is not for sale!"

B.B. leaned in close, until our **WHISKERS**

touched. We stared at each other snout-to-snout. Finally, he burst out, "I know who you are! You are the editor of The Rodent's Gazette! How much do you want for your newspaper? How much would it cost to take it off your paws?"

I stared him down. "Sir, you can add The Rodent's Gazette to the list of things that you cannot buy!"

"Is that so, **Mr. Big-Shot Editor Mouse**? Yours truly *can* and *will* buy whatever I like!" he hissed. "And I'll do it, or my name isn't Bradley Bigbottom!"

Then he left.

At that moment, Oswald came running up. His fur was as white as a bowl of milk. **"The ghost is coming! Run! HEEEELLLLLLP!"**

A GHOST TRAP!

The ghost howled, *"Get ooouuuuut of heeeere, all of yooouuuuu! Thiiiiis iiis myyy hotellllllllll!"*

But the ghost didn't get far. Hercule and I scurried right up to him and ripped the helmet and wig off his head. Underneath we saw … **Ms. Bertha!**

Only then did some of the strange particulars of the case come back to me. First of all, Bertha looked a lot like Bradley Bigbottom. Although she was tall and stout and he was short and thin, she had the same **EXPENSIVE** tastes as he did … and she also wore the initials B.B.!

Then I understood. She was actually Bertha Bigbottom, **Bradley Bigbottom's sister!**

GET OUT OF HERE,
ALL OF YOU ...
GET OUT OF HERE,
ALL OF YOU ...

Bertha Bigbottom

Who she is: A very tall and very stout lady mouse who is always dressed elegantly. She is clever and quite snooty.

What she does: She is quite a capable manager. What does she specialise in managing? Anything – as long as she's in charge!

Her plan: She and her brother Bradley are in cahoots with Sleezer, a wicked rodent who wants to take over Mouse Island. In exchange for helping, Bertha wants to become president of Mouse Island.

Her secret: She longs to conquer Sleezer's heart.

Her dream: To become the most powerful rodent on Mouse Island!

Her weakness: She is a very greedy mouse.

Bradley Bigbottom

WHO HE IS: A VERY SHORT AND VERY THIN MOUSE. LIKE HIS SISTER, HE IS CLEVER AND ALWAYS ELEGANTLY DRESSED.

WHAT HE DOES: HE IS A SHADY TRADER AT NEW MOUSE CITY'S HARBOUR. WHAT DOES HE TRADE? ANYTHING – AS LONG AS HE CAN TAKE A BIG CUT!

HIS PLAN: HE IS SLEEZER'S RIGHT-PAW MOUSE. HE WANTS TO HELP HIM TAKE OVER MOUSE ISLAND. HIS PRICE: ALL THE GOLD IN ALL THE BANKS ON THE ISLAND.

HIS SECRET: HE IS A MASTER OF SPECIAL EFFECTS.

HIS DREAM: TO BECOME THE RICHEST RODENT ON MOUSE ISLAND!

HIS WEAKNESS: HE CAN'T RESIST CHEDDAR-FLAVOURED CHOCOLATES.

WHAT A KLUTZ!

"**Bravo!** You rodents are heroes for solving this mystery!" Horatzio exclaimed.

"I'll tell you who the real hero is," Hercule exclaimed. "My dear friend Geronimo Stilton!" He reached over to hug me but accidentally **stuck** his finger in my eye.

"Ooooouuuuuuuuuchhhhhh!" I squeaked.

"Uh-oh, did I hurt your eye? I'm so sorry!" Hercule shouted.

He took me by the paw and led me to the revolving door ... which my tail got caught in!

"Oooouuuuuuuuchhhhhh!" I screeched.

Hercule brought me an ice cube for my hurt tail, but he dropped it. I still couldn't see because of my swollen eye, and I slipped on it!

"Yeee-oouuuuuuuuuchhhhh! I've broken my leeeeeeeeeeggg!" I cried.

"Call 999!"

Luckily, someone had listened to me, and an ambulance soon arrived.

I winced in pain as the doctor checked me out. "Yes, sir, it seems that you have broken your leg."

That Hercule Poirat!

What a klutz!

WATCH OUT FOR THE CAAAAST!

At the hospital, they put a cast on my leg. Then they sent me home.

The next day, Hercule Poirat paid me a visit. I could tell he was feeling guilty.

"My dear Stilton, I hope you're surviving," he said anxiously. He pawed me a box of BANANA-FLAVOURED chocolates. Ugh, I detest bananas. Then he tripped ... and **grabbed** my leg to keep from falling!

"Ooowwwww!" I yelled. *"Watch out for the caaaast!"*

"**SORRY** SORRY SORRY, Stilton!" he cried. Then he repositioned my leg on a pawstool and took out a pen. "I'll sign it!"

As he bent over, he slipped and **SMASHED** his snout into the cast.

"Oooowwwwwww!" I yelled. *"Watch out for the caaaast!"*

Hercule sprang to his paws again. "Sorry sorry sorry, my dear Stilton!" Then he opened up the box of chocolates. "Yum-yum-diddly-dum!" he exclaimed with satisfaction. He began shovelling chocolates into his snout. He was eating so ferociously, he **KNOCKED** over the table ... which hit me on the leg.

"Ooowwwww!" I yelled. *"Watch out for the caaaast!"*

Hercule scrambled back to his paws. "SORRY sorry sorry, my dear Stilton!"

I propped myself up on a crutch so I could see him to the door.

At that moment my sister Thea arrived ... on her

motorcycle! "Howdy, big brother! Aren't you happy to see me?"

As she squeaked, she **RAN** into my leg with one of the motorcycle's tyres.

"Ooowwwww!" I yelled. *"Watch out for the caaaast!"*

I sank back down into my pawchair.

Just then my cousin Trap arrived. He gave me a big, hearty **SLAP** on my cast. "So, it's really broken, huh? You're not faking it?"

"Ooowwwww!" I yelled. *"Watch out for the caaaast!"*

Then my grandfather William Shortpaws showed up. "Geronimo, where did you break the BONE? Here or here?" he asked, tapping my leg energetically. "Squeak up, grandson!"

"Ooowwwww!" I yelled.

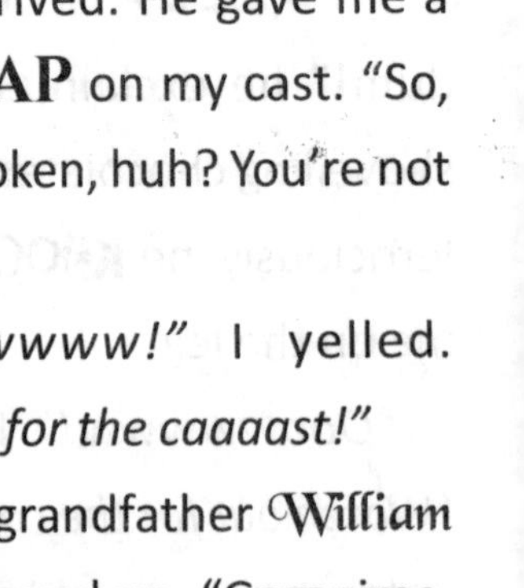

"Watch out for the caaaast!"

Next my friend Creepella strolled in, along with her pet bat Bitewing, who immediately **dove** for my leg.

"Ooowwwww!" I yelled. *"Watch out for the caaaast!"*

Then came Bruce Hyena, shouting, "Ready for a little physical therapy, champ? I'll get you back in shape in no time! I'll have you exercising day and night!"

He did push-ups on one paw but he lost his balance and **HIT** my leg.

"Ooowwwww!" I yelled. *"Watch out for the caaaast!"*

Finally, my editorial assistant, **Pinky Pick**, came skipping in with a radio playing at full blast. "Boss, feel like dancing?" she cried exuberantly. She pulled me up and I tried

hobbling around on my crutch, but then she **stepped** on my paw.

"Ooowwwww!" I yelled. *"Watch out for the caaaast!"*

I fell back into my pawchair just as my nephew Benjamin came in. He took one look at the crowd and cried, "Stop it, everyone! Let Uncle Geronimo rest!"

I hugged him gratefully. "Thank you, Benjamin. **You're the only one who understands me!**"

Guess Who the Guest of Honour Is?

Horatzio came in just as Benjamin was trying to usher everyone out. "Geronimo, my old friend! Now that you and Hercule have **unmasked** the ghost, I would like to invite all of New Mouse City to the Grand Hotel tonight for a great MASQUERADE BALL! Guess who the guest of honour is!"

"I-I-I don't know," I stuttered.

"Why, it's *you*, Geronimo Stilton! Who else could it be?" Horatzio cried.

I stammered, "B-but I can't possibly attend, my leg is in a cast ..."

"I have a genius idea!" Hercule exclaimed. "You can dress up as a MUMMY! The bandages will go perfectly with your cast."

"Quite right, Mr. Poirat!" cried Grandfather William. "That is a genius idea!"

"I could do with a little less genius around here," I muttered. But no one paid any attention to me. The next thing I knew, Hercule had **WRAPPED ME** in bandages from snout to paw. Just like a mummy! So I was forced to attend the great masquerade ball. The whole city was there, in the Grand Hotel's **BALLROOM**.

As everyone was dancing the Swiss Cheese Shuffle, I looked out the window. The moon was shining in the sky, illuminating the rooftops of my sweet New Mouse City.

OH, HOW I LOVED THIS TOWN!

There were so many familiar places: the station, the theatre, the library, and the art mouseum. I could also see the cheese market, Singing Stone Plaza, and *The Rodent's Gazette* offices, and all the way on the horizon was the airport.

I felt tied to all the rodents who lived here, as if our lives were connected by **STRING CHEESE**!

This adventure had truly reminded me that there are things that just cannot be bought, like the memories, events, and traditions at New Mouse City's Grand Hotel. **It's a place I'll carry in my heart forever!**

THE RODENT'S GAZETTE

1. Main entrance
2. Printing presses (where everything is printed)
3. Accounts department
4. Editorial room (where editors, illustrators, and designers work)
5. Geronimo Stilton's office
6. Geronimo's botanical garden

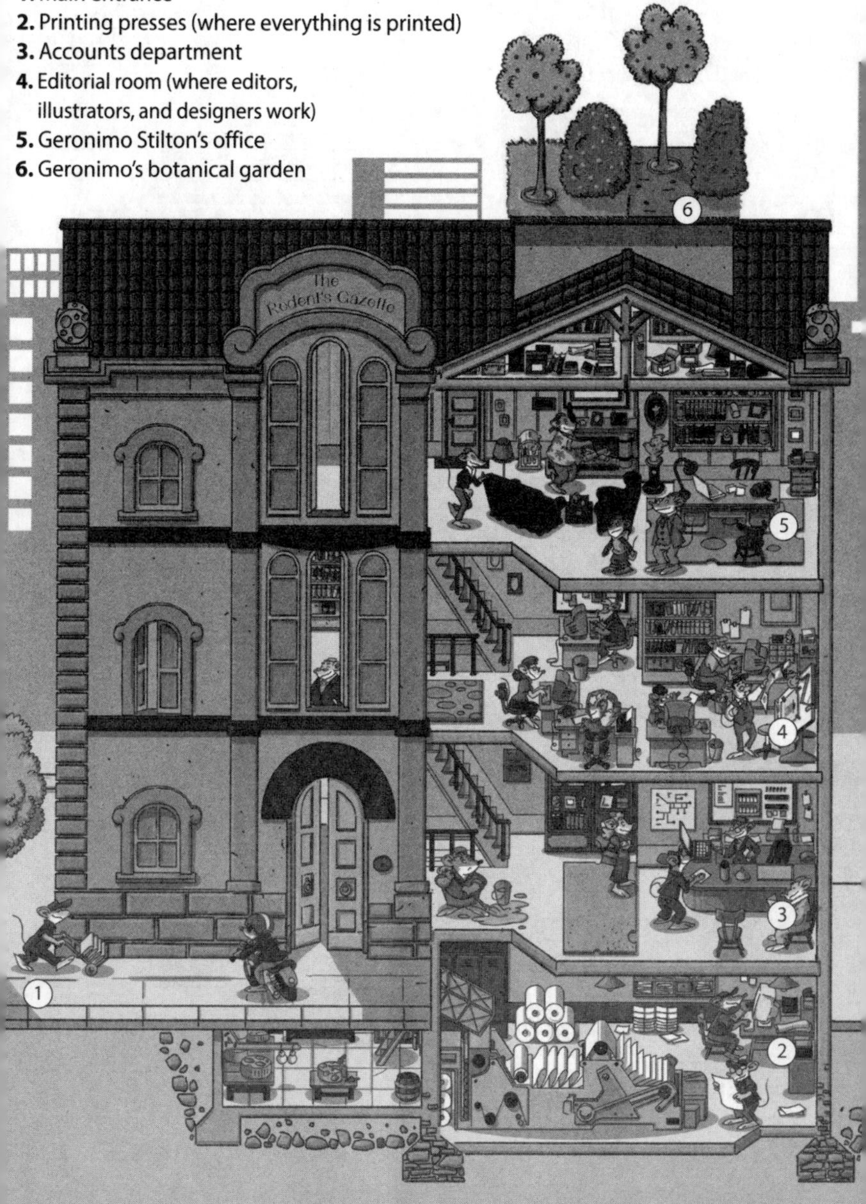

9
1
2
18
4
8
3
12
32
13
11
10
19
45
5
22
46
20
15
17
7
40
24
26
25
28
33
38
27
36
14
16
23
37
31
21
29
44
35
41
30
34
6
42
39
43

MAP OF NEW MOUSE CITY

1. Industrial Zone
2. Cheese Factories
3. Angorat International Airport
4. WRAT Radio and Television Station
5. Cheese Market
6. Fish Market
7. Town Hall
8. Snotnose Castle
9. The Seven Hills of Mouse Island
10. Mouse Central Station
11. Trade Centre
12. Movie Theatre
13. Gym
14. Catnegie Hall
15. Singing Stone Plaza
16. The Gouda Theatre
17. Grand Hotel
18. Mouse General Hospital
19. Botanical Gardens
20. Cheap Junk for Less (Trap's store)
21. Parking Lot
22. Mouseum of Modern Art
23. University and Library
24. The Daily Rat
25. The Rodent's Gazette
26. Trap's House
27. Fashion District
28. The Mouse House Restaurant
29. Environmental Protection Centre
30. Harbour Office
31. Mousidon Square Garden
32. Golf Course
33. Swimming Pool
34. Blushing Meadow Tennis Courts
35. Curlyfur Island Amusement Park
36. Geronimo's House
37. Historic District
38. Public Library
39. Shipyard
40. Thea's House
41. New Mouse Harbour
42. Luna Lighthouse
43. The Statue of Liberty
44. Hercule Poirat's Office
45. Petunia Pretty Paws's House
46. Grandfather William's House

MAP OF MOUSE ISLAND

1. Big Ice Lake
2. Frozen Fur Peak
3. Slipperyslopes Glacier
4. Coldcreeps Peak
5. Ratzikistan
6. Transratania
7. Mount Vamp
8. Roastedrat Volcano
9. Brimstone Lake
10. Poopedcat Pass
11. Stinko Peak
12. Dark Forest
13. Vain Vampires Valley
14. Goosebumps Gorge
15. The Shadow Line Pass
16. Penny-Pincher Castle
17. Nature Reserve Park
18. Las Ratayas Marinas
19. Fossil Forest
20. Lake Lake
21. Lake Lakelake
22. Lake Lakelakelake
23. Cheddar Crag
24. Cannycat Castle
25. Valley of the Giant Sequoia
26. Cheddar Springs
27. Sulphurous Swamp
28. Old Reliable Geyser
29. Vole Vale
30. Ravingrat Ravine
31. Gnat Marshes
32. Munster Highlands
33. Mousehara Desert
34. Oasis of the Sweaty Camel
35. Cabbagehead Hill
36. Rattytrap Jungle
37. Rio Mosquito
38. Mousefort Beach
39. San Mouscisco
40. Swissville
41. Cheddarton
42. Mouseport
43. New Mouse City
44. Pirate Ship of Cats

1
2
3
4
5
6
7
8
9
10
11
12
13
14
15
16
17
18
19
20
21
22
23
24
25
26
27
28
29
30
31
32
33
34
35
36
37
38
39
40
41
42
43
44

THE COLLECTION

HAVE YOU READ ALL OF GERONIMO'S ADVENTURES?

- ☐ *Lost Treasure of the Emerald Eye*
- ☐ *The Curse of the Cheese Pyramid*
- ☐ *Cat and Mouse in a Haunted House*
- ☐ *I'm Too Fond of My Fur!*
- ☐ *Four Mice Deep in the Jungle*
- ☐ *Paws Off, Cheddarface!*
- ☐ *Fangs and Feasts in Transratania*
- ☐ *Attack of the Pirate Cats*

- ☐ *A Fabumouse Holiday for Geronimo*
- ☐ *Hang on to Your Whiskers*
- ☐ *School Trip to Niagara Falls*
- ☐ *The Christmas Toy Factory*
- ☐ *Geronimo Stilton, Secret Agent*
- ☐ *A Fantastic School Adventure*
- ☐ *The Cheese Experiment*
- ☐ *The Super Chef Contest*
- ☐ *Welcome to Mouldy Manor*
- ☐ *The Treasure of Easter Island*
- ☐ *Mouse Overboard!*
- ☐ *This Hotel Is Haunted*

ABOUT THE AUTHOR

Born in New Mouse City, Mouse Island, GERONIMO STILTON is Rattus Emeritus of Mousomorphic Literature and of Neo-Ratonic Comparative Philosophy. For the past twenty years, he has been running The Rodent's Gazette, New Mouse City's most widely read daily newspaper.

Stilton was awarded the Ratitzer Prize for his scoops on *The Curse of the Cheese Pyramid* and *The Search for Sunken Treasure*. He has also received the Andersen Prize for Personality of the Year. His works have been published all over the globe.

In his spare time, Mr. Stilton collects antique cheese rinds and plays golf. But what he most enjoys is telling stories to his nephew Benjamin.